WALT DISNEY PICTURES

TARAN
AND THE
MAGIC
CAULDRON

formerly released as "THE BLACK CAULDRON"

TARAN'S MAGIC SWORD

A GOLDEN BOOK • NEW YORK

Western Publishing Company, Inc., Racine, Wisconsin 53404

Long ago, in the land of Prydain, a boy named Taran lived with his old guardian Dallben. Taran loved danger and adventure. But much as he longed to be a great warrior, he still was only the pig-keeper in Dallben's barnyard.

"Dallben thinks I'm too young to be a hero," Taran muttered as he carried food to Hen Wen the pig. "If only I had a proper sword, he'd see that nothing could stop me."

More than anything, Taran wished for a chance to fight the evil Horned King who threatened Prydain. "Until that chance comes," he thought, "this big billy goat will have to do."

"Even the Horned King shakes with fear," Taran laughed, rattling the goat's horns with his stick.

"Stop your fooling and give Hen Wen a bath," Dallben called from his cottage.

But almost as soon as Taran got Hen Wen in the water, she began to squirm and squeal.

"What's wrong, Hen?" Taran asked. "Usually you like having a bath."

"What's going on out there?" Dallben called.

"It's Hen Wen," Taran replied. "I can't keep her still. She's trying to get away!"

"What?" Dallben gasped. "Quickly, my boy, bring her inside."

"You are about to see something that you must never reveal to anyone," Dallben warned Taran. He set a pan of water before the pig. "I've never told you, but Hen Wen has magic powers."

Dallben swirled the water with his stick. Hen Wen stuck her nose in the water as Dallben recited a spell. Wavy images began to form in the pan.

"There's the Horned King," said Dallben. "And there's the Black Cauldron!"

"What's the Black Cauldron?" Taran asked.

"It's a terrible weapon, and the Horned King must never find it. If he does, he'll destroy the world!" Dallben broke the spell. "Take Hen Wen away from here," he said. "If the Horned King were ever to capture her, he would make her show him where the Black Cauldron is hidden."

"This is the chance I've been waiting for," Taran said as he led Hen Wen through the forest. "Action! Adventure! I'll be the greatest warrior in all Prydain! I'll protect you from the Horned King, Hen Wen . . . Hen Wen? . . . HEN WEN!"

Taran had been so busy boasting that he had not seen Hen Wen wander off. He searched and searched for her.

But Taran found the pig too late. An iron-clawed
gwythaint swooped down from the sky and snatched Hen
Wen up. It carried her off to the Horned King's castle.
"I'll save you, Hen Wen," Taran promised. "I don't
know how, but I will!"

Running as fast as he could, Taran finally reached the Horned King's gloomy castle. He climbed the sheer stone wall and crept through the winding passageways. Taran found a hiding place in the rafters of the huge dining hall.

Even the rafters shook when the Horned King entered the room.

"Bring in the prisoner," came the command.

A guard led Hen Wen before the Horned King's throne. Taran trembled as the Horned King tried to make Hen Wen tell him where the Black Cauldron was hidden.

Taran had to stop him. He had to stop the guards from hurting poor Hen Wen.

"No! Don't!" Taran yelled, tumbling from his high perch.
He grabbed Hen Wen and ran from the room.

Hastily, Taran carried Hen Wen to the top of a high tower, then pushed her over the wall. Hen Wen fell into the moat below and swam across. Then she scampered away.

But there was no escape for Taran. Strong arms grabbed him from behind, and he was thrown into a deep dungeon.

There he sat, his head in his hands. "I guess Dallben was right," he sighed. "I'm not much of a hero. First I let them capture Hen Wen. Now here I am, locked up forever."

Just then a strange ball of light appeared in the cell. It darted from place to place. Taran looked up in surprise.

He was even more surprised to see what followed—a pretty girl, just his age. "Who are you?" Taran asked.

"I'm Princess Eilonwy," the girl replied. She pointed to the ball of light. "That's my magic bauble."

"I am Taran the pig-keeper," Taran said.

"My bauble and I are going to escape," said Eilonwy. "If
you want to come along, you may."

"Let's go!" Taran cried.

Together they made their way through the dungeon's
twists and turns.

Around a corner, Taran and Eilonwy came upon a statue of a great king holding a mighty sword. Taran slipped the sword out of the statue's grip.

"The statue isn't going to need this sword," Taran said. "But maybe we will."

His new sword raised, Taran led the way.

In another part of the dungeon, Taran and Eilonwy
found a poor minstrel. The Horned King's guards had
chained him up and left him in the dark prison.

"I am Fflewddur Fflam," the minstrel said. "I will sing far
and wide of the Horned King's wicked deeds."

"We'll have you unchained in a minute," Eilonwy
promised.

But the Horned King's guards were upon them. "Hurry, hurry!" Fflewddur urged as the friends separated in the dungeon's winding tunnels.

A guard trapped Taran in a corner, and brought a huge
ax crashing down. Taran held up his sword and . . . *clang!*
The ax shattered.

"It's magic!" Taran gasped. "A magic sword!"

Eilonwy, who had seen everything, ran to Taran's side. "Are you all right?" she asked.

"Come on!" Taran replied. His sword easily beat back every one of the cruel guards in their path.

Still more guards were coming after them. Taran and
Eilonwy kept running, and soon they found themselves in
the wine cellar.

With his sword, Taran poked holes in the huge barrels
of wine. The Horned King's guards slipped and slid on
the wet floor.

"Catch me if you can!" Taran dared them. They couldn't
catch him. With Fflewddur at their heels, Taran and
Eilonwy ran out of the castle and into the woods.

"You were very brave, my boy," Fflewddur told Taran gratefully.

"I always knew I could be a hero!" Taran said happily.

Then, with the magic sword at his side, Taran set off with his friends to find and destroy the Black Cauldron. He was more determined than ever to keep Prydain safe from the evil Horned King.